ELOP'S STORY

A YOUNG ARTIST IN ANCIENT TIMES

Story and Illustrations
By

WILLIAM H. CHRIST JR.

Copyright © 2021 William H. Christ Jr.

All rights reserved. No part of this book may be reproduced in any form or by any electronic or mechanical means, including information storage and retrieval systems, without permission in writing from the publisher, except by reviewers, who may quote brief passages in a review.

ISBN: 978-1-63795-730-1   (Paperback Edition)
ISBN: 978-1-63795-731-8   (Hardcover Edition)
ISBN: 978-1-63795-729-5   (E-book Edition)

Some characters and events in this book are fictitious. Any similarity to real persons, living or dead, is coincidental and not intended by the author.

Book Ordering Information

Phone Number: 315 288-7939 ext. 1000 or 347-901-4920
Email: info@globalsummithouse.com
Global Summit House
www.globalsummithouse.com

Printed in the United States of America

Dedication

For the late Sister Anna Mae

Teaching Sister from The Daughters of Charity

Professor, Art Historian and Mentor

ELOP'S STORY

A YOUNG ARTIST IN ANCIENT TIMES

Story and Illustrations

By

WILLIAM H. CHRIST JR.

Once upon a time in a faraway land of ice and snow lived a young boy named, Elop. He, his family and friends were members of a small clan of human wonderers.

The time of this story is probably more than ten thousand years ago, near the end of the last great Ice Age. The people were nomadic and moved across the desolate frozen parts of northern Europe, searching for good shelter and a constant food supply.

By today's standards, those people were very primitive. They were, however, able to make fire and use stone tools. Stone points on sticks and wooden clubs became weapons for hunting. They fashioned animal fur into clothing and bedding. Their lives were simple and quite short. Age thirty was considered old in their time due to the harsh conditions under which they lived.

Elop was a boy of eight years and was strong and full of life. His father Grok, was nearly twenty-five, and considered the leader of this particular Clan of people. There were about a dozen families in the clan. All the families had several young children.

Words were spoken in a crude way. Usually the person speaking would hold an object and make a sound to mean what the object was or did. Nothing was written down for there wasn't any alphabet nor paper at that time. All the clan members used the same sounds for the same objects. Elop already knew many of the adult sounds which made his parents proud.

Both the adults and the children were very superstitious. They had little understanding of their world, only nature's rules. Often, they were afraid of the unknown and would run and hide. The clan members believed that weather conditions, animal migrations and the changing of the seasons all were the result of some magical or spiritual power.

Elop liked playing with the other children in a frozen forest. They played hide and seek. The boys often pretended to hunt wild animals like the ones in the stories told by their fathers. The young girls preferred to remain close to their mothers. They learned about cooking and caring for their families in their makeshift huts.

Elop was a curious boy, and often wandered off alone to explore new things. He was also a star gazer, spending countless hours lying on his back watching the stars, wondering what made some blink and some to shoot rapidly across the sky.

Clouds fascinated little Elop. How do they change shape, what makes some white, some gray and some golden? He loved all the colors in the clouds. His world was mostly white with snow and ice.

* * *

One day, little Elop and some other boys entered a small opening in the side of a rocky outcrop. The small space soon opened into a large underground room. The place felt warm and safe.

"Our whole clan would be able to live in this nice space," he thought to himself. The boys reminded Elop that this place was a long distance from where the clan members had set up their huts. The boys stayed in the cave for several hours. They found that there was a stream which ran through part of the cave. Without fire, the boys could not explore the cave thoroughly so they left to return to their huts.

Elop did not know how to tell his parents about the cave. He thought and thought. When he arrived back at the huts, he found three stones. He placed one stone on top of the other two leaving an opening which was the object that everyone knew meant a cave.

Seeing the stones, Elop's father called the other clan adults together. They agreed this would be a good place to live. Little Elop was very happy that the adults understood his object.

Soon, the entire clan had taken down their huts and walked the long distance to the rock outcrop. Grok and the other men cautiously entered the underground cave with fire sticks. The clan elders lit up one large room after another. The men agreed this would become their new home. Children excitedly entered the cave along with their mothers and their personal belongings.

* * *

Things went well with the new "Cave Dwellers" until their food supply began to run low. The clan elders decided it was time for another hunt. No one had seen any large animals near the cave since the clan had moved in. They knew they would have to travel far on foot.

Little Elop was sad since he was still too small to go with his father on the hunt. Tearfully, he and the other children watched as the elder men sharpened their stone tools and weapons and left the cave for the hunt.

The men left footprints in the snow which the children followed for a short distance until near sunset. They then hurried back to their cave before dark. Elop wondered when the hunters would return.

* * *

Many days and nights passed and the food supply dwindled to nearly nothing. All the children felt hungry. The mothers searched daily for simple grains, berries and some honey. This simple food would sustained the clan until the men returned from their hunt.

* * *

Little Elop became thinner as the days passed without meat to eat. He longed to taste the roasted meat as he stared at the few burnt sticks lying at the edge of the fire pit. His little hand reached down and picked up one of the sticks. One end of the stick was burnt black. Elop touched the burnt end and the black came off onto his fingers. He became upset and tossed the stick across the cave's room. The stick hit the cave wall and made a long <u>BLACK</u> line.

Elop ran over to the wall and picked up the stick. He then made some more black lines with his stick, on the cave's stony wall.

"This is fun," he thought to himself. "What would happen if I just moved the black lines together?" He did, and the marks combined into a familiar shape.

"It looks like a deer's head with antlers!" he exclaimed.

Kneeling down, to the cave's floor, Elop took some of the reddish-brown dirt and rubbed it onto his deer head.

"The color's just right," he thought. The young boy stepped back to admire his drawing of a deer head with antlers.

"Something's still not right," he said shaking his shaggy head of hair. He then hurried back to the flickering fire pit. He quickly gathered several more burnt-ended sticks, and returned to the cave wall. The fire in the pit gave him light and cast eerie-looking shadows on the walls around him.

Soon, little Elop had drawn the rest of the deer's body ...even its tail! The drawing looked great but he, on the other hand, looked a real mess. His hands, face and feet were black from the burnt wood and the rest of his hair and clothes were covered with the reddish-brown dirt. Elop didn't realize his appearance until his mother pulled him by the ear to the underground stream. She held up a fire stick so he could see his reflection in the water.

She pulled his clothes off and pushed him into the cold water!

Little Elop slept soundly that night after his big day of firsts...making his first drawing on the cave wall and taking his first real bath!

* * *

Excitement filled the cave as the hunters returned. The men had traveled far and were weary. The hunting was difficult and they brought less than half the meat of what the previous hunt had yielded. Elop was so happy to see his father that he gave him a big bear hug. That night, a huge fire burned in the fire pit. Everyone in the clan ate roasted meat and it was delicious.

After the feast, the men told stories about the hunt to their wives and children. As the fire grew less, the mothers put the sleepy children to bed.

That night, as Elop slept, he dreamed of seeing herds of different animals: deer, bison, wooly mammoths and even ferocious saber-toothed tigers!

* * *

Earlier, Grok had noticed the deer drawing on the cave wall. He was impressed and asked, "Where did this come from?" None of the elders knew of its origin. Grok felt this was a "Good Sign."

* * *

The following day, the children played outside the cave while Elop returned to the fire pit room and began drawing and coloring more animals on the cave walls. By the end of the day, he had many different size and shaped drawings of deer and bison.

As Elop was about to leave the fire pit room, Grok entered and said loudly, "My son! You did these?"

Little Elop was afraid since his father was so big and strong. Lowering his head and expecting to be punished, he softly said, "Yes, father. I did this."

His father knelt down and held out his large hand saying, "Teach me. I, too, want to make the animals. It is a good sign...I am sure, my son."

Little Elop didn't know what to say, so he gave his father another big bear hug.

* * *

During the next several months, Elop showed his skill throughout the cave's many rooms. Together with his father, they decorated each room with animal drawings and scenes of the hunt. The drawings were colored with all earth tone colors found inside the cave. There were YELLOW, RED, <u>ORANGE</u> and <u>BROWN</u> clays along with <u>WHITE</u> chalk and the <u>black burnt wood</u> called, <u>Charcoal</u>.

The clan members liked the drawings on the cave walls. Each time they would leave the cave, they noticed the temperature becoming milder. Soon, all the snow and ice began to melt.

* * *

One night, little Elop awoke to the sound of running water. "The cave is flooding!" he cried out.

Everyone quickly grabbed their belongings and moved to higher ground. The little stream inside the cave became a raging river! The swift running waters completely erased all the wall drawings!

ELOP'S STORY

Elop cried as his father told him that the wonderful drawings, they had made, were gone. Sobbing, he told his father, "You said the drawings were a good sign, but the evil one has destroyed them."

"Maybe they were good after all. Look for yourself, son," his father told him. Little Elop wiped away his tears and looked outside of the cave. He could hardly believe his eyes.

Whole herds of deer and bison appeared very close to the outcrop rock. They had come to graze on the newly growing grasses that had been buried under the snow and ice.

* * *

Elop's clan continued to live for many years in the cave beneath the outcropped rock. As he grew to become a hunter, Elop also became an excellent artist. He painted new drawings of the animals and the hunt scenes on the ceilings of the cave. That way, the spring floods never washed them away.

Elop never signed his art masterpieces, but he often included his hand print on the cave ceiling for all the clan members to see.

More than ten thousand springs, summers, falls and winters have come and gone since Elop drew animals on the cave ceilings. Recently, some young school-age children and their collie dog were playing in a friendly farmer's field. Near one corner was a rocky outcrop.

The collie suddenly disappeared from their sight. The children called and called for their collie. They ran to the pile of rocks at the end of the field and could hear their dog barking. Moving some rocks, the collie jumped out and the children could clearly see an entrance to an underground cave.

Excitedly, they asked the farmer to help them explore the cave. He agreed.

With the farmer's flashlights, the collie led the way as the children and the farmer carefully entered the cave. Once they could stand upright, they found themselves inside a large underground room!

When the farmer shone his light onto the cave's ceiling, there was a squeal of joy from the children and the dog began barking. Directly over their heads were hundreds of beautiful drawings, in <u>EARTH-TONE COLORS</u> of ancient animals. Pictures also showed the men who hunted them for their food, and hides for clothing. Each picture was made from Black, Brown, Orange and White colors found inside the caves.

* * *

Carefully climbing onto a rocky ledge, each child compared the small archaic hand print with their own.

* * *

Art is used today in making designs for our Computers, Internet, television, space travel, world-wide communications and a continuing growing appreciation of the Fine Arts. Art today is found everywhere, and in every country around Our World. Art is very importance in our lives. We each see it on even on some of the clothes we are wearing! Art: <u>HISTORY</u>, <u>DESIGN</u>, <u>LOGOS</u>, <u>ADVERTISING</u>, and <u>ARCHITECTURE</u>, all started out when a little "Cave Dweller" from the <u>STONE AGE</u> tossed a burnt stick against his cave wall and drew the first LINE_____.

The End

Can You Draw a Picture like Elop did and attach it here?

Can You Draw a Picture like Elop did and attach it here?

Can You Draw a Picture like Elop did and attach it here?

Can You Draw a Picture like Elop did and attach it here?

Can You Draw a Picture like Elop did and attach it here?